"We knights do not min a big job.

We might even see a  DRAGON ,"

says Sir  TYRONE .

"Brave knights, I must go to the  store.
I need a new ," says King .

The BACKYARDIGANS™
Follow That Egg!

adapted by Catherine Lukas
based on the original teleplay by Adam Peltzman
illustrated by The Artifact Group

Ready-to-Read

SIMON SPOTLIGHT / NICK JR.
New York   London   Toronto   Sydney

Based on the TV series *Nick Jr. The Backyardigans*™ as seen on Nick Jr.®

SIMON SPOTLIGHT
An imprint of Simon & Schuster Children's Publishing Division
1230 Avenue of the Americas, New York, New York 10020
© 2008 Viacom International Inc. All rights reserved.
NICK JR., *Nick Jr. The Backyardigans,* and all related titles, logos, and characters are trademarks
of Viacom International Inc. NELVANA™ Nelvana Limited. CORUS™ Corus Entertainment Inc.
All rights reserved, including the right of reproduction in whole or in part in any form.
SIMON SPOTLIGHT, READY-TO-READ, and colophon are registered trademarks of Simon & Schuster, Inc.
Manufactured in the United States of America
First Edition
2 4 6 8 10 9 7 5 3 1
Library of Congress Cataloging-in-Publication Data
Lukas, Catherine.
Follow that egg! / adapted by Catherine Lukas ; illustrated by The Artifact Group. —1st ed.
p. cm. — (Ready-to-read)
"Based on the TV series Nick Jr. The Backyardigans as seen on Nick Jr."
ISBN-13: 978-1-4169-5040-0
ISBN-10: 1-4169-5040-0
I. Artifact Group. II. Backyardigans (Television program) III. Title.
PZ7.L97822Fo 2008
2007007529

"Look! King  has
PABLO

a job for us," says  .
TYRONE

"Ready, Knight  ?"
UNIQUA

"Ready, Sir  !"
TYRONE

"I know! Maybe King  PABLO

needs us to go up DRAGON MOUNTAIN,"

says Knight UNIQUA.

"Your job is to take care of this 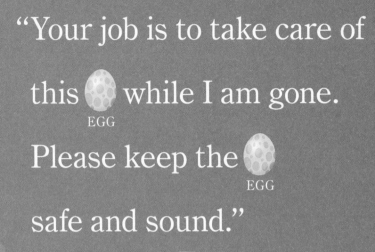 while I am gone. Please keep the EGG

safe and sound."

"An 🥚?" asks 🐰.

EGG · UNIQUA

"An 🥚 does not move

EGG

at all," says 🫎.

TYRONE

" 🐉 ⛰️ would be more

DRAGON MOUNTAIN

interesting."

The 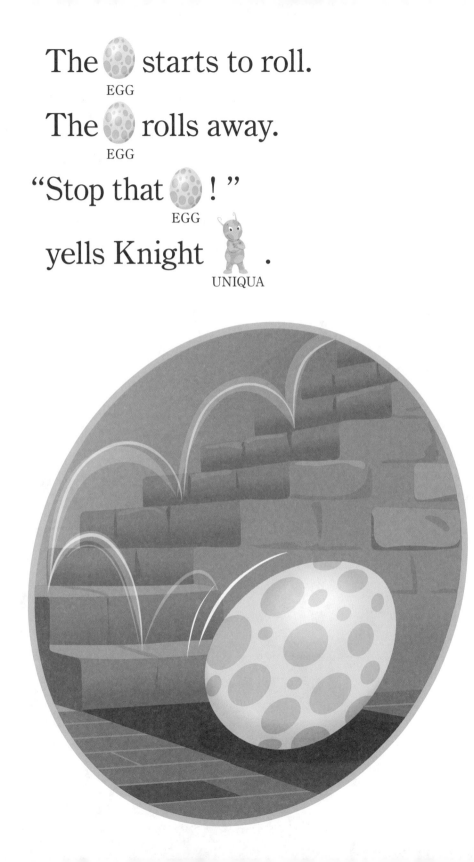 starts to roll.
EGG

The 🥚 rolls away.
EGG

"Stop that 🥚 ! "
EGG

yells Knight 🐜 .
UNIQUA

The  rolls
EGG

down the [STEPS] ,
STEPS

through the [DOOR] ,
DOOR

and into the [WATER] .
WATER

The 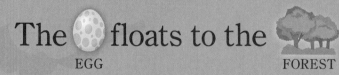 floats to the
EGG   FOREST
of the Grabbing Goblin.

"The Grabbing Goblin

will grab the !" says
EGG

Knight .
UNIQUA

"Watch out!"

Someone grabs

their ,
HELMETS

their ,
SHIELDS

and then the !
EGG

"Grabbing Goblin!"

says Knight .
UNIQUA

"Give back that !"
EGG

It is too late.

They all go over

the  .

WATERFALL

Hooray! They catch the 🥚!
EGG

Crack!

Now the 🥚 has 🦵!
EGG   LEGS

The 🥚 runs away.
EGG

They pass the Fairy .

Fairy  wants the  too!

She tries to take it.

Crack!

Now the EGG has WINGS!

The EGG flies away.

It flies up DRAGON MOUNTAIN.

"The 🥚 is in danger!"

EGG

says Fairy 🦛 .

TASHA

"Oh, no! What if a 🐉 gets it?"

DRAGON

asks Sir 🦌 .

TYRONE

"We have to save the 🥚 !"

EGG

At the top of  DRAGON MOUNTAIN,
Sir TYRONE finds an empty
shell. Did the EGG hatch?

"Ah! A DRAGON !" yells AUSTIN.

"Run!"

They run. Then they fall.

A baby  catches them.

DRAGON

"Look what hatched from

the  !"

EGG

says Knight  .

UNIQUA

"We have to show the king!"

says Sir  .

TYRONE

King  returns.

PABLO

He has a new 👑.

CROWN

"I see the 🥚 hatched,"

EGG

he says.

"I hope it was no trouble."

"Not for brave knights like us!"

says Sir  .

TYRONE

"Good," says King  .

PABLO

"I knew you could do the job.

Come to my  for a snack!"

PALACE